RULERS OF A DEAD PLANET

BY RYAN WOLF

An imprint of Enslow Publishing
WEST 44 BOOKS™

**Please visit our website, www.west44books.com.
For a free color catalog of all our high-quality books,
call toll free 1-800-398-2504.**

Cataloging-in-Publication Data
Names: Wolf, Ryan
Title: Rulers of a dead planet / Ryan Wolf.
Description: Buffalo, NY : West 44, 2026. | Series: West 44 MG verse
Identifiers: ISBN 9781978597990 (pbk.) | ISBN 9781978597983 (library
bound) | ISBN 9781978598003 (ebook)
Subjects: LCSH: Imaginary places--Juvenile fiction. | Siblings--Juvenile
fiction. | Imaginary wars and battles--Juvenile fiction. | Extraterrestrial
beings--Juvenile fiction. | Planets--Juvenile fiction.
Classification: LCC PZ7.1.W654 Ru 2026 | DDC [F]--dc23

First Edition

Published in 2026 by
Enslow Publishing
2544 Clinton Street
Buffalo, NY 14224

Copyright © 2026 Enslow Publishing LLC

Editor: Caitie McAneney
Cover Design: Leslie Taylor

Photo Credits: Cover, series art (main cover image & interior stars) p. 5,
25, 37, 49, 124 AI image composite/Shutterstock.com; p. 74 (alien hand)
Illizium/Shutterstock.com, (child hand) Eladora/Shutterstock.com; p. 141
Magician ART/Shutterstock.com; p. 146 Agungru/Shutterstock.com.

All rights reserved. No part of this book may be reproduced in any form
without permission in writing from the publisher, except by a reviewer.

Printed in the United States of America

CPSIA compliance information: Batch #CS26W44: For further information contact
Enslow Publishing LLC at 1-800-398-2504.

For Autumn and Ronan,
little explorers of the universe.

With special thanks to
Caitie McAneney,
Ian and Kelly Richardson,
and my family.

Translated from Noburan Records

The Noburan Code

Honor the many wonders of the many worlds.
Draw out what is good from the ground.
Call down what is great from the skies.
Stir the depths for hidden light.
Bring life from death.

Obey the path of wisdom.
Study its map and know its ways.
Show caution and care in every act.
Test for truth in times of shadow.
Remember what is right.

Teach order to the chaos.
Tame the wild wastes of senseless space.
Let peace flow from star to star.

SO?

I'm not sure
why we pretend
some stupid code
has all the answers.

I Have some PROBLEMS WITH IT

The Noburan Code
doesn't give very clear directions.

It doesn't tell us anything
about the places where
we set our ships
and build our bases.
Digging and scraping.
Pushing and planting.
Growing the future.

Though it's not like
I'm part of the projects anyway . . .

I spend most days
trapped behind curved metal.
Listening through
the flaps in my neck
for any sign that
I'm even wanted here.

BOREDOM

The air is stale
in the silvery halls.

    A low pulse beats
    from the screens
    on the softly glowing walls
    of my podroom.

        Boredom lives inside
        every upload
        I get from my Illumi-Pillow.

            Empty facts.
            Pointless lessons.
            Beamed into my brain
            when I lay my head to rest.

I can't do anything
with the things I learn.

My parents won't let me.

THE ROYAL NOBURANS

My father and mother.
Lord and Lady.
They're rulers
of this dead planet.

Every planet we visit
is at least half-dead.

But our workers
break through the crust.
Pulling richer minerals
to the surface.

They tend to seeds
designed by Noburan scientists.
Speeding their growth.

The budding plants
meet the
special demands
of each world
they're made for.

My mother loves to manage
the garden domes
where the experiments begin.

She treasures the ripe rows.
Hanging vines.
Sweet fruits.
Veined petals.
Bright leaves.

      Colors blooming, burning, bursting.

My father is more about
numbers and charts.

He takes in data points
on each new planet.
Tracking weather.
Studying wildlife.
Sampling soil.
Testing for radiation.

      Finding patterns, problems,
      possibilities.

Vorlarus, his grand advisor,
maps out zones
with his robotic drones
and reports back.

Depending on how things look,
our scientists might tinker
with the atmosphere.
Create chemical clouds.
Change the weather systems.

They want the planet
to be as friendly for life
as possible.

Once a planet is deemed safe,
other Noburans can move in.

We hope to spread our ways
of grace and peace
to every livable land.

But *peace* might just be
another word for *boring*.

naRVU, MY BROTHER

He doesn't care
about our parents' projects.

I care.
It's just that
no one cares that I care.

Most planets have
beasts that bite
and poison plants
and falling rocks.
So I'm not allowed
outside to explore.

I'm not old enough
to run the gardens
or fly the drones
or mix the stormy chemicals.

If I were Narvu,
I'd be happy with
the shimmery hologames
projected from our podroom walls.

But I like things that are *real*.

SORT OF . . .

I like to *imagine*
the cracked desert
beyond our base.

Maybe my imagination isn't *real*.
But it feels more real
than the hologames
with their laser lines.
Preset grids.

I hear there are towers
buried in the desert.
Their tops stick up
like crooked spikes
from the dry ground.

They're all that's left
from the creatures
that ruled this world before us.

I sometimes wonder what they looked like . . .

SHAKING, QUAKING

The glow-panels
on my walls
rattle.

The deserts of
my imagination
dissolve.

Tremors trickle
along the floor.

Earthquakes,
Grand Advisor Vorlarus
calls them.
Plates of rock
shifting beneath us.

They've broken
parts of our base before.
Nothing repair crews
can't fix though.

I almost wish
the quake
would rumble louder.

I almost wish
the windowless walls
would tumble down.

There's so much to see
beyond my little cell
of a room.

FLICK-FLICK-FLICKER

The glow-panels blink on-off-on.
Switching colors rapidly.
Like they're sending panicked signals.

"Nuh-nooo,"
Narvu howls
from his podroom.

His hologame must have restarted.

"I was so close,"
he groans.

I'm not sure if
he's trying to talk to me
or the game.

"It's not real,"
I tell him.
"That game doesn't count
for anything, Narvu."

"You don't count
for anything, Nulara,"
my brother half-hisses,
half-shouts back.
"I had one more base
to build . . ."

"Then what?"
I ask,
rushing through the hall
from my room to his.
"You'd just play
the same game over again."

"But isn't that what we do?"
Narvu asks
as I appear beneath
his arched doorway.
"The game's basically
a Noburan training exercise.
You hop from world to world.
Take it over.
Make it better.
Move on to the next one."

"It's not the same . . ."
I try to convince Narvu
(and myself).
"There's actual dust
to get on your boots out there . . .
Risk and chance
and mystery and—"

"You've got a head full of comets,
don't you, sis?"
Narvu snarls,
cutting me off.

He shuts down his game grid.
Rolls back all three
of his bright yellow eyes
into their scaly lids.

"We obey the path of wisdom,"
he says.
"Not the path of risk
and chance and mystery
and being a mega-mess
of a meteor-mind."

He knows
I want to sneak out.

I don't even have to say it.

Narvu is about to call me
more nasty names.

His tongue freezes instead.

The ground grumbles.
Louder than ever before.

Narvu's body jolts.
His neck fins wiggle.
Fluttering with fear.

Flick-flick-flicker.

All the lights
go out.

emergency

When the power is on,
the security doors
are impossible
to get through.
The gates demand
six-finger scans.

With the power off,
we can lock and unlock doors
on our own.

Our parents
don't want us trapped
in an emergency.

This could be
an emergency.

Couldn't it?

excuses

"What if the base
is really-really broken
this time?"
I ask Narvu
as backup beams
switch on.
"What if our parents
are in danger?"

Narvu's eyes narrow.
His scales drain
from blue green
to purple gray.

"I'm not going outside,"
he says.

Shaking, quaking.

C r a c k i n g.

One of the panels
in Narvu's podroom
splits down the center.

Sparks sail
from the screen.
Streaming out
in an electric shower.

Narvu leaps away
from the flare
and the flash.

His eyes aren't
so narrow anymore.

"Sure you want
to stay here?"
I ask.

My webbed mouth
barely holds in
bubbles of laughter.

IN OUR GRAVI-SUITS

We check the comms
on our armbands first.
Try connecting with our parents.

But the bands won't work.
The power outage
must've knocked out
our communications.

Nobody's come racing in
to see if we're alive.
We have to look out
for ourselves.

Hopefully,
we've put our spacewear
on correctly.

The Gravi-Suits
are puffy and saggy.
Too big for us.

Compared to the robes
we usually wear,
they don't fit very well.

But everything is
sealed up tight.
The suits can recycle
the air we breathe.
We don't need to worry
about it running out.

Though the comms are down,
Narvu and I can chat
through headsets behind our visors.
Our suits carry speakers.

"Ready?"
I ask my brother.

Instead of answering,
Narvu turns up his visor's tint.
It goes from clear to black.

Shading out his face completely.

AT THE DOOR AT THE END OF THE WIDE, WINDING HALL

We twist the override latch.
There's a buzz as it opens.

Inside is a station
for spraying our suits
when we return.
A place to clean off
the planet's filth.

Long-necked nozzles
lean over us.

We walk past them.
Toward another door.
Smaller and rounder.
Bordered by dull backup lights.

The next latch
is the most important one.

another Twist and a Buzz

The circular door rises.

White blazes
into our visors.

I quickly tint mine
to match Narvu's.

My middle eye
takes longer to adjust
than the other two.
It's sharper.
More sensitive.

What it finally takes in
is much more
disappointing
than I'd hoped.

WHEN WE FIRST LANDED

I was asleep on the ship
in my freezer-bed
during our touchdown.

Workers carted
my cold body
to a base-bed on land.

In the morning,
my Illumi-Pillow sent
electro-jabs to wake me.
I felt so heavy and sunken.
Still tired somehow.

My parents weren't there to greet me.
Narvu was already
in the middle of a hologame.

I was on a new planet.
But I could've been on the last one.
Or any one of ten before that.

MY DISAPPOINTMENT

The desert before me is barren.
No towers in sight.
Only gray skies,
and gray ground
patched with
dark, glassy rock.

There's not
a murmur of mystery
or the invitation
to any adventure.

Just endless gloom.
Wild waste
in senseless space.
Winds sweeping off
to nowhere.

"Turn around,"
says Narvu.

BEHIND ME

On the other side
of the base.
Casting shadows
on our halls and domes.
Bending over us.

A dead city.

The burnt frame
of a lost world.

Melted metal
folds in triangles.
Molten mounds
are fused together.

Though I can't see
his face beneath
his visor, I
wonder
if even Narvu
finds this
exciting.

As I gaze at him,
my brother
drops his head.
Looks at the ground
nearest to us.

Cracks from
the earthquakes
branch and spiral.
Tagging the sides
of our base.

We should head
toward the garden dome.
See if anyone is hurt.

That would be
the noble Noburan
thing to do.

But I know
where I want
to go instead.

"HEY!"

As Narvu chases after me,
I skip-hop over
the quake-cracks.
Thrusters on my pack
propel me forward.

They get my feet
just high enough
to make it feel like
I'm flying
for a moment.

Dust blasting up
from beneath
keeps getting caught
in the pipes on my pack.

Still the city
creeps closer-closer-closer.

Narvu won't drag me back.

CITY OF ANCIENT ANIMALS

I touch the black column
of a burned-out building.

Weird beasties crawled
inside these ruined walls.
Ages ago.

SMACK.

I hit the column head on.

Narvu has slammed
my shoulders
with fury and force.

Now he's punching
the sides of my visor.
Knocking on
its screen.

I shove him off.

He rolls onto
a rippled sheet of metal.
Hidden in the dust.

It's oddly loose.

As he slides sideways,
Narvu's right boot
dips into
a gap in the ground
beside the sheet.

Narvu shrieks
as if he's falling
off a cliff.

He springs
to his feet.

He throws out
his arms.

He lifts up
the rippled sheet.

a DISCOVERY

It's a hatch
of some kind.
Inside,
a smooth tunnel
drops downward.

"Helloooo?"
Narvu calls into the shaft.

He's not showing
caution and care.
Not like the good Noburan
he's supposed to be.

To anyone who
doesn't understand our language,
his call must sound
like one long squeal.

Our raspy headsets
don't help any.

PEERING IN

A ladder runs
down the side
of the opening.
Disappearing
into the dark.

As I touch it,
the ladder shakes.
My gloved fingers
can't get a grip.

I tumble into
the shaft.
Diving down
the unknown tunnel.

The walls
slip away
in a blur.

Narvu shouts something
as I fall,
but I can't hear it.

I click for
the thrusters
on my pack.

They spurt out dust.

       Jammed.

Down
I
go.

AT THE BOTTOM

Before there's time to worry,
I land with a bounce.

My boots
toss me upward.
Then I flip
back down in a heap.

The surrounding chamber is dim.
Yet not as dark as expected.

Discs holding tiny lights
are spread around
a dirty room.
They show
the shadow-shapes
of furniture.
Blocky objects
I have no names for.

Something lives here.

I am not alone

I hear a shuffle.
Spin around.

In a corner,
beside a glowing bar,
sits the strangest thing
I've ever seen.

The beast is gray.
Covered in what
must be ash.
Dressed in crusty rags.

A monstrous head
pops up from between
the creature's arms,
which cradle a set of thick legs.

It has two eyes
with green rings
circling inside them.

They're white as a star
on the outside.
Black as space
in their centers.

The glaring eyes
hang right above
a big bulge of skin
with holes in it.

Below curl
two meaty red flaps
that open to reveal rows
of pale little rocks.

The thing is what
my Illumi-Pillow
labels a "mammal."
On the top of its head
is a stringy patch of fur.

I have no idea why
random fur would grow
in such a bizarre place.

It looks like
an ugly helmet.

Stepping back,
I almost press
the button to send
a shock wave
from my armband.

This would strike
the beast
down.

It's a wild animal
after all.

Who knows what
the things
on this planet
might do?

Then I look
into the rings
of the animal's eyes.

THE EYES OF THE BEAST

There is
something sad
in the creature's gaze.

Something that
wants more than
it knows.

Something that
reminds me
of myself.

MERCY FOR A MONSTER

The ashy beast
is so tiny next to me.

It could be a child.

I lower the tint
on my visor.

When I do,
I can tell the critter
thinks I'm terrifying.

As I loom over it,
it covers its mouth
with a five-fingered hand.

"It's okay,"
I say.

Hearing my voice
makes the animal flinch.

The phaser on my armband
is called a "weapon of peace."
There's even a *SOOTHE* setting.

Sometimes my father
uses it on himself
to help him relax.

It seems to work
on most lifeforms.
I could calm the beast.

But I'm not sure if I need to yet.

I hold out my dusty glove.
There's no gift inside my palm.
Yet this feels like
the right motion.

The creature timidly reaches
with its own hand.
It pulls back
when it hears Narvu
shout for me.

"I'm still alive,"
I call upward.
"We have a friend down here."

"An animal friend?"
Narvu asks from above.
"Pets aren't allowed."

"Obviously,
we can't bring it back,"
I say,
keeping my eyes
on the creature.
"But I don't think
it's going to eat us."

"It could shoot quills
or spray acid
or burp blue flames,"
Narvu says,
panic in his voice.
"Come up and we'll tell
the Grand Advisor.
He'll know what the beast-thing is."

I'm still mad at Narvu
for hitting me.
And I don't want
to go back to the base.

But what if the creature
is hiding something?
What if it's more of a threat
than it appears?

As I scan the chamber,
I see other doorways.
Lined with glowing bars.

Halls stretch into unseen rooms.
There must be more of these
short, scaleless monsters.

They're smart enough
to build bunkers
and hang lights.

I'm not equipped
to deal with them.

So I give in.
I back toward the ladder.
Steady and slow.

The creature's eyes
keep tracking me.
It looks more curious
than frightened now.

I give a Noburan goodbye
to the little beastie
by wiggling
both of my arms.

The ladder clink-clangs
as I bump it accidentally.

Then I turn.
Climb-climb-climb.

Narvu is leaning
over the opening.

I push him away
when I reach
the top.

"Sorry for attacking you,"
he says.
"But we can't leave
the base like that."

I hiss through my headset.
Kick at the dust.

My brother doesn't deserve
a better response
than that.

LEAVING

We keep the hatch uncovered
so Grand Advisor Vorlarus
can find it easily.

We should probably
tell him about
our discovery
right away.
Though I don't
exactly want that . . .

As we march
toward the base,
I glance back.

I want to take in
the dead city
one more time.
To dream of
its underground secrets.

As I turn,
I catch sight of
that ugly helmet of fur.

The little beastie
is poking its head
out of the hatch.

It's squinting.

Watching us
drift away
into the dreary desert.

RETURNING

By the time we reach the base,
the comms are on again.

Which means
the outer gate is locked.

We'll have to
ask our parents
to let us in.

I was hoping we'd just talk
to Grand Advisor Vorlarus
about the animal.

He makes me uncomfortable.
But he usually won't
tell our parents
if we misbehave.
He'd rather not get involved.

I know Narvu will blame everything
on me . . .

TIP-TIP-TAP

Narvu is about
to call up our parents.
But the sound of footsteps
makes him pause.

When we spin around,
the creature from the chamber
is squatting behind us.

This is Narvu's first look at the beastie.
He staggers backward in shock.

To my surprise,
the animal makes
a gurgled noise
that must be a laugh.

I see its belly bobbing.
It wiggles its arms playfully.
Mimicking the way
I said goodbye.

Narvu has set
his armband weapon
to *STUN*.

I signal for him
to lower his aim.

"I don't think
there's anything to fear,"
I say,
still hoping
the thing's friendliness
isn't a trick.

The creature points
to one of the cracks
from the quakes.

It makes a motion with one arm.
Rolling it like a wave.

Then it crinkles its face.
Like it's pretending
to be scary.

"What's it doing?"
Narvu asks
nervously.

"Maybe it's a game?"
I guess.
"Or maybe it's saying
something about
the earthquakes?"

The creature
repeats its motion.
There's an urgency
to whatever message
it's sending.

As if it wants
to warn us.

THE DOOR OPENS SUDDENLY

Grand Advisor Vorlarus
is at the gate.

As the tallest Noburan on base,
he's easy to spot.
I can also see
his grim green face
through his visor.

Vorlarus breathes heavily
into his headset.

"What are you doing?"
he asks us,
stretching out each word.

Narvu and I
stumble after
an explanation.

"The p–p-power was out,"
I stammer.

"Nulara made me go with her,"
Narvu says.
(Which isn't quite right.)

The Grand Advisor
doesn't react.
He just lets us
keep tripping
through our excuses.

"We wanted to see if
our parents were okay,"
I tell him.
"Then we saw the city
and we wondered
if they might be in there—"

"Not true,"
Narvu interrupts.
"Nulara wanted to
run in and—"

"Well, Narvu attacked me,"
I interrupt in return.
"That's not
the Noburan way . . ."

The silence of
the Grand Advisor
makes me trail off.

"We found a lifeform,"
I say,
changing the subject.

I point behind me.
Thinking the creature
must still be there.

But when I look,
our new friend is gone.

HUH?

"It was just here,"
I insist.
"The beast-thing
basically tried
to talk with us."

Narvu backs me up.

"It was a stubby mammal
that walked upright,"
he says.

Vorlarus calmly
lifts his armband
to scan the area.

"There shouldn't be any lifeforms
of that kind here,"
he says,
sending out
a web of thin laser lines.

Bright blue rays
spill out over the desert.

"There are creatures
in the city,"
Vorlarus continues,
sweeping his lasers
from left to right.
"We caught spiky-shelled beasts
out here earlier.
Six-legged monsters
as high as my waist."

"We didn't see any of those,"
I say.
"These ones had two eyes.
They had fingers and head-fur
and stood on two feet."

"Humans? Here?"
Vorlarus asks,
clearly alarmed.

He stops the scan.

HUMAN HISTORY

"I don't know
what the animals are called,"
I say.
"My Illumi-Pillow hasn't
told me anything."

"Humans are the mammals
that built this city,"
Vorlarus says.
"They're also the ones
that blew it up."

I have trouble imagining
the creature we saw
destroying anything.

"There aren't many humans left,"
Vorlarus goes on.
"They mostly live in caves now.
That's the reward they get
for destroying their wonderful world . . ."

"What did their world
look like before?"
Narvu asks.

"It was a place of great beauty,"
Vorlarus replies.
"Lush life abounded.
Through valleys and hills.
In untamed jungles
and well-farmed fields.

But they dropped
too many bombs at once.
They threw their perfect planet
into a long, dark season.
An age of brutal cold.
Nuclear night.

Smoke veiled the sky.
Radiation ruined the soil.
Most plants and animals
went flat-out extinct.
Countless chains of living creatures
were lost forever."

This is so far from
the Noburan way
that it's hard for me
to understand.

"Why would they do that?"
I ask.

"The humans couldn't get along,"
Vorlarus says.
"In the name of fighting evil,
they wiped out
every good thing
they ever had."

I think of my brother and myself.
Tussling in the dust.

Our spats aren't that bad.

But what if they were?

What Vorlarus says next
doesn't give me any comfort.

DUE FOR DESTRUCTION

"The humans are children of war,"
the Grand Advisor tells us.
"Those who delight in death
will find what they seek.

I've run through models
of possible futures.
I believe the path of wisdom
is hard,
yet clear.

It takes us to only one place.

For the safety of this planet,
we'll need to remove
any humans that remain.

We must destroy them
completely."

SERIOUSLY?

This seems extreme.
But the Grand Advisor is sincere.

"Let me show you
what the humans did,"
he says.
"It will be a lesson.
You shouldn't wander out
into a land of killers.
Your parents want you
indoors for a reason."

I'm not sure what
is about to come next.

Vorlarus presses on his armband.
Instead of scanlines,
a warped, wavy hologram
projects outward.
It fills the shape and size
of the city itself.

"This is a chrono-capture,"
explains Vorlarus.
"It's the closest you'll get
to time travel.
We use historic heat patterns
in the region.
The images you see
are just an outline.
But I don't think you'll like them."

Narvu leans forward.
He lowers his visor tint
to see a bit better.

This is like one of his hologames.
At the scale of an entire skyline.

"I'm setting the chrono-capture
to the moment with
the greatest thermal energy
in its databank,"
Vorlarus says.

Whatever that means.

HEAT GHOSTS

A picture appears
in the wavy light.
It washes over
the jagged landscape.

Fallen buildings
sprout up like stalks.
Their broken bodies
shoot skyward.
As if they're bolting out of bed.
Fleeing a bad dream
they finally awoke from.

The skyline seems filled with
mighty towers.
Their beams are no longer bent.
They're healthy and strong.

Their checkered windows remind me
of the scales on my own body.

But they're only ghosts.

WHAT WAS LOST

Metal boxes on wheels
charge through busy streets.

Winged animals soar in the air.
Some perch on wires.

Trees line the roads.
Branches brimming with leaves.

There are so many humans.
A bustling sea of life.
Rippling in holographic waves.

They seem to know
where they are going
and what they want.

They don't look like
a species that's about to
destroy themselves.

THE SCENE EXPLODES

A white flash
appears in the distance.
Then a fiery avalanche
blazes and rolls into the city.

The scalelike windows
s h a t t e r.

Flames punch through them.

Glass pops out
into a burning,
surging stream of fire.

The humans have disappeared.

The towers are tumbling
into the firestream.

The image blurs
into a thick cloud of smoke.

THE PICTURE FADES

Vorlarus dials down
his projection.

The living city vanishes.
A dead one has taken its place.
Returning us to
the present moment.

"Should a species
that does *that*
be allowed to continue?"
Vorlarus asks,
lowering his arm.
"What else might it do?"

FUTURE HORRORS

The thought of animals
like the one I met underground
being harmed,
by themselves or by others,
makes me sick.

"Humans killed other humans,
so your answer is to
kill *every* human?"
I ask the Grand Advisor.

Narvu whips his head toward me.
He doesn't like this question.

"They also killed off
other species if you recall,"
the Grand Advisor says.
"They could hurt
future Noburans."

He has a point.

MY PARENTS

The Lord and Lady
are quick to agree
with their advisor
about the human problem.

They're even quicker
to punish
their rule-breaking kids.

They're locking down
our podroom doors.
"Grounding" for us
is like going to prison.

Unfortunately,
I was wrong about Vorlarus.

Because of the safety risk we took,
the Grand Advisor
felt he had to report us.

He doesn't want us
getting attacked by humans.

At the same time,
he *does* want us
to show him where in the city
we found the humans' nest.

He's hoping
we'll get "ungrounded"
to help with his hunting.

Our mother and father
won't allow that.

They tell Vorlarus
to use his drones
to scout the area.
To forget about us.

We're both in real trouble.

And it's (mostly) my fault.

THE BLAME LANDS ON US BOTH

My father looks at
his children
like a math problem
he can't solve.

"We just want you to be safe,"
he says,
pinching the ends
of his purple robe.
"That's all . . ."

My mother blinks at us
with her large, lovely eyes.

"We expected more of you,"
she says,
making my soul
feel shrunken
and small.

LOCKED AWAY

My podroom feels
more lonesome than ever.

Our parents had
all our screens and projectors
shut off.

This must be especially
hard on Narvu.

Usually,
I talk to him through
the walls of my room.

Now he won't
speak to me.

NOTHING TO DO

Illumi-Pillows are
the only tech we can use.

I lie in bed.
Try to download info about humans.
The system won't let me.

But when I ask
the pillow about war,
I'm flooded with tales
of terrible battles
across far-off galaxies.
Seems humans aren't
the only enemies of life.

While words and images
crackle into my brain,
I feel movement
that isn't from the pillow.

Something is shuffling beneath my bed.

THE KILLER

As I jerk my head
in the direction of the noise,
the human from the hatch
springs out.

The creature looks cleaner
than I remember.
Both its body and clothes
seem washed and dried.
Like they were
hosed down
at the spray station,
then fanned off.

When Vorlarus left the base,
the human must've
snuck behind him.
Entering through
the just-opened gate.

Since we were
outside for so long,
the crafty critter
had plenty of time
to get clean,
then hide away.

We probably
sprayed our own suits
right next to the beastie.
It crouched
behind supplies.
Spying on us.

When we were done,
it followed us
into our halls.

And now it's in
my podroom.

Using those sad eyes
to make me feel bad for it
all over again.

I'M NOT AFRAID

There's nothing scary
about the thing
in front of me.

After everything I've learned,
I still don't hate
this weird beastie.
Even if its species
might harm us.

The human coughs.
It can breathe
the atmosphere
in our base.
But not well.

It moves a finger
toward my middle eye.
I can tell as a two-eyer,
it finds three eyes funny.

I put my hand
in front of my face
so the human doesn't poke me.

My hand is twice as big
as the little thing's head.

It touches its own hand
to my finger-scales.
Runs it up and down
my palm.

The pressure
is so light.

I should scream
for someone
to save me.
Tell the Grand Advisor
to set his armband
weapon to *SLEEP* mode.
Fire-fire-fire.

But then
he'd never
let this human
wake up again.

THIS IS a
meGa-mess

I'm sure this beast-thing
must be a kid.
It's hopping around my room now.
Patting and pushing
on the wall panels.

When it tries to touch
my Illumi-Pillow,
its fur frizzes up.

Power flowing from the pillow
shocks the creature.
Its eyes create liquid.
A clear trickle runs
down its cheeks.
It tries not to wail.

I touch the human-child's left cheek.
Its eyes stop leaking.

The creature cups my wrist.

now i'm scared

The human-child starts
wagging my hand
up and down.

Then it reaches for the fins
on the sides of my neck.
Grabs and pulls.

The tugging hurts.

I push on the finlike things
the human must use
for its own hearing.
They feel a lot harder
yet bendier
than my neck-flaps.

The human-child giggles
through the holes
in the pointy peak
at the center of its face.

QUAKING, SHAKING

The human scurries back
as the floor sways.

A rumble and a roar
rise from below us.
Like an explosive
was tested underground.

This is the loudest,
angriest tremor yet.

All the panels in my room
begin cracking.
Splitting apart
into shards.

The human hides
under my bed frame.
Staring upward.
Waiting for the ceiling
to fall.

The ribbed metal covering
over us is secure.

Still,
I join the creature
beneath the bed.

We wait through the rumbling.
Coming in wave after wave.

*Is this even
an earthquake?*

The human-child does
a rolling motion with its arm.
It's the same motion
from earlier.

The kid makes the same
pretend-scary face
it did before.

But this time,
I'm actually scared.

UNGROUNDED

My podroom door
    is suddenly
        ripped away.

        Like a cyclone

           is sucking it

        into the void.

FIRE TAIL

A sparking surge of electric white.

As bright as the bomb in the
human city.

But whipping like a wild wind.

A diamond tail
swiping away
everything
in its path.

THE FLAMEBEAST

It rises up
to the place
where my door once stood.

It shimmers
as it slithers back
into a pit.

The ground has broken
to reveal a chasm.

White fire
whirls
within it.

A flaming braid blasts
through the space
where the hall was.

I'm worried about my brother.

smoke spreads

I call for Narvu.
But I can barely speak
as the planet's air
pours into the base.

There's a gash in the ceiling now.
Part of the metal is bent back.
Revealing the gray sky above.

I start gagging.

The human-child
seems to understand.
It races to the rack
where I keep my Gravi-Suit.

Once the suit is in my hands,
I breathe deeply into the helmet.

My head feels lighter.

I SPEAK INTO MY HEADSET

Narvu?

Narvu?

Put your suit on, Narvu.

Put your suit on!

at First there is silence

Then I hear a rustling from
where Narvu's room should be.

There's a zipping sound.

With a crick-crackle,
Narvu's headset comes to life.

"Thanks, Nulara,"
he says.
"I'm alive.
Though I don't know
how long either of us have . . ."

"What was that thing?"
I ask,
hoping my brother had
a clearer view of
the firebeast.

"I think it's the end
of everything,"
he whispers.

THE RUMBLING STOPS

The human-child
crawls forward.
Stands up.

It slinks over
to the chasm.

The creature
makes a sign for me
to follow it.

Then it waves
to Narvu's room.

I hear my brother squeal.

I know he's seen
the human now.

NARVU JOINS US

My brother is
less trusting than I am.

But we both follow
the human-child
along the edge
of the chasm.
It seems to know
how we can get out.

The kid guides us
carefully around
the wreckage.

The base is
beyond battered.
It's torn open.
Shredded on all sides.

I'm afraid to think
about my parents . . .

OUTSIDE

Smoke pushes skyward.
Swirling out
from burning buildings
across the base.

I feel fear tickling
underneath my neck-flaps.

Things look almost as bad
as in the chrono-capture
Vorlarus showed us.

Only the garden dome
seems untouched.

Hoping my parents
are in there,
I bound in that direction.

The human-child
yanks me back.

BENEATH A MELTED WHEEL

There's another hatch.

The human-child pulls off
the warped metal.
It shows us the ladder
to another tunnel.

Are these passages
even safe
with a firebeast
roaming underground?

If the monster
can break apart
a Noburan base,
it can crash through
human tunnels.

Can't it?

RUSHING DOWN
A DIM HALL

Round red lights
dot the tunnel.

Drawings mark
the walls.
Images repeating
themselves
in different orders.

These could be
symbols from
a human alphabet.

I hope the beings
that made these tunnels
have answers.

I hope the people
our people want dead
will save us.

enTERInG a WELL-LIT CHamBER

At the end of the tunnel
is a room with
three walls.

Each side of the triangle
holds a different path.

In the center is
a cluster of glowing bars.

The poles give off
a blue light.

At first,
I think the bars are fixed.

Then the human-child
plucks one out.
It sticks the blue bar
out like a spear.

FINDING THE ADULTS

The human child
takes us down a tunnel
with a letter from
the human alphabet
written over the entrance.

Soon we're in a new chamber
where I catch sight of
more humans.

These ones
are taller and wider.
Their skins
carry different shades.
Some have long manes.
Some aren't furry at all.

But they're all much scarier
than the child.

And far less friendly.

aRe we PRiSonerS?

The two-eyed stares
of the grown-up humans
make my scales shake.

Narvu tries
to speak with them.
But they plug up
their head-flaps
with their fingers.

They can't handle
the noise coming from
his headset.

"I want out of here . . ."
Narvu cries
helplessly.
"I want my mother . . ."

WE NEED TO GO

I decide to test
whether or not
we're actually prisoners.

I bolt toward
a tunnel exit.

Narvu scrambles after me.

Racing, racing.

We enter the same chamber
I found earlier in the day.
Take the ladder up.
Move the rippled sheet.

And there we are.
Inside the ruined city.

There's no one behind us.

BUT . . .

In front of us,
it's a different matter.

There's a red-orange,
six-legged,
spiky-shelled,
oversized insect-beast
of death and doom.

Basically what Vorlarus
mentioned earlier.

It scuttles over to Narvu and me.
Drawing apart its giant pincers.

> I swerve my head
> and duck.

The bug clamps onto Narvu's helmet.
Scratches and scrapes the visor.
Clacking as it strikes.

SHOCKING THE SPIKESHELL

Now is the time
to use my "weapon of peace."

I raise up my arm.
Select *STUN*
to stop the insectoid.

Electricity flows
from my armband.
Shooting into
the spikeshell's side.

The creature doesn't seem to notice.

It keeps pecking away
at Narvu's helmet
as my brother
kick-kick-kicks.
Struggling
to get free.

SLIPPING

I feel something seize my right leg.
Then slam me down.

Another of the spikeshells is behind me.
Grabbing my boot.
Trying to pierce my suit.

I twist and fire again.
This time with SLEEP.

    Nothing.

SOOTHE.

    Nothing.

SLAY.

    Nothing.

The spikeshell drags me along the dust.

ITS PINCERS ARE ALL I CAN SEE

They're on my helmet now.
Prying at the visor.

I push-pull-push
with all my might.

Trying
to
break
them away.

But when
I finally do,
I see there's another spikeshell
behind the one
I'm fighting.

And another creeping beyond that.

The first spikeshell
goes for my visored face again.

BLOWN away

Bits of shell
strike my helmet.

A smoky hole appears
in the spikeshell's side.

It falls onto
its back.
Legs wriggling.

I slide sideways.
Snatch up my brother.
Just as the spikeshell
on top of him
gets blasted backward.

We dodge
chunks of ground
that spurt around us.

As we almost reach
the hatch opening,
I notice the humans.

They're outside the hatch.
Firing shiny, sparky black tubes.

Whatever's in them
is powerful enough
to fight off
the insectoids.

After another round
of popping
from the tubes,
the spikeshells flee.
Skittering away.

At least the ones
that are still alive.

BACK IN THE HATCH

We hurry down
the ladder.

The human-child is
in the chamber.
Still grasping
the glowing blue spear.
Peering at me
in a way that's
hard to read.

I see a few other humans
gripping their own glow-spears.
They use the pale light
to get a better look at us.

These humans saved our lives.

And I don't know why.

THE GLOW-SPEARS LOWER

The humans must not know
what to make of us yet.

If they knew what
the Noburans were planning,
would they have rescued us?

One figure with a black tube
comes down the ladder behind us.
It has tufts of fur
around its rocky mouth.

Its eyes look tired.
Its cheeks are streaked with dust.

It wears scrap metal
to protect its chest.
The armor is dotted
with dents and dings.

This must be a leader of humans.

THE LEADER SPEAKS

I don't understand
the sounds that slip
from the human's mouth.

The animal has
a low, grumbly voice
that reminds me of the earthquakes.

It gives some type of order.
Bodies move when it shouts.

A line of humans with glow-spears
take off down a tunnel.

I see other humans
carrying babies.
Kissing their foreheads.
Holding them close.

They head down
a different hall.

THAT LEAVES NARVU AND ME

What do our rescuers want with us?

We can't make sense
of the leader's barking.

The human-child
brings over a sheet
with images on it.

There are ashy drawings
of the firebeast.
The creature looks like
one long crinkled tail.

In the picture,
the humans surround the firebeast
with their glow-spears.

Whatever material is in the spears
must keep the monster back.
Out of the tunnels.

no PROTECTION

Our base doesn't have
the materials that the humans do.

I can already imagine
the firebeast
smashing through
the glass of the garden dome.

Crushing the plants.
Snapping the trees.
Lighting our parents aflame
in their royal robes.

Their high status
won't save them.
And our status
won't save us.

Only the humans can.

I WANT TO TELL THE LEADER THIS

But I think
it already knows.

It points
to the drawings.
Points to us.

And points up
to the light
at the top of the ladder.
Just as a whirring sound
appears over
the hatch opening.

I see a sleek shape.
Glossy black
and full of blinking buttons.

The drone
lowers itself
into the chamber.

VORLARUS

The Grand Advisor
has found us.

I recognize his drone right away.

Two more drones
follow the first.
Buzzing their way
into the room.

The leader aims a tube
at the nearest drone
and fires.

It *pings* the device.
Glints off.

The human-child
bats at a drone
with its glow-spear.
That doesn't drive it back.

Instead,
the drones continue to swarm.
Darting about the chamber.

They stand in each corner.
Clinking and whirring
louder now.

A gray mesh jets out
from the drones.
Trapping the humans
in nets that tighten over them.
Squeezing to match
their exact shapes.

The leader's weapon
smacks its head
as a net
sucks into its skin.

The human-child
hugs its glow-spear,
which pokes out
of another net.

It cuts itself away.
Dropping to
the floor.

The other drones
are already
taking their prey
out of the hatch.

The bagged bodies
bang against the ladder
as they're lifted up.

They disappear
through the hatch-hole.

The human-child screams.

It reaches
its chubby arms
toward the opening.
Which soon
is blocked by shadow.

STUNNED

The Grand Advisor
fires an electric pulse
at the child.

It falls to the ground.
Shocked.

The armband phasers
might not work on the spikeshells.

But they're sure effective
against humans.

I touch the child
on its shoulder.
Making sure
it isn't hurt too badly.

"Away from the animal,"
Vorlarus snaps.

SOOTHED

I send calming pulses
into the child's head-flaps.

"I said leave the human boy alone,"
Vorlarus howls.
"Don't make me
shoot him again."

Stepping away
from the fallen creature,
I face the Grand Advisor.

"The humans rescued us,"
I say.

"*I'm* rescuing you,"
Vorlarus growls.

"Nulara's right,"
Narvu butts in.
"She's telling the truth."

THANKS, BROTHER

I'm surprised to see
Narvu defending me.

Even he seems to think
the Grand Advisor
is going too far.

"We've got to
save our parents,"
I say,
hoping Vorlarus will listen.
"Only the humans know
how to beat the firebeast
who destroyed our base."

"Firebeast?"
Vorlarus smirks,
knowing more than we do.
"Humans created
the Atomic Serpent."

THE ATOMIC SERPENT

"Humans are the source
of every evil on this planet,"
Vorlarus spits.
"As they developed
better ways to kill each other,
they did awful experiments
on their fellow animals.
They created new kinds
of radioactive life.
Some of the creatures they made
still haunt the desert."

I hold up the human-child's
wrinkled drawing.

"So you knew
about this Atomic Serpent?"
I yell at the advisor.
"You knew it would
attack our base?"

"I knew of the serpent
by studying human history,"
Vorlarus admits.
"I didn't know
it was causing the quakes.
I didn't know it was here."

"Do you know how to fight it?"
I ask.
"Do you know
how to keep it away?
The humans can help us."

"The humans will kill us,"
Vorlarus says,
pointing at the crumpled child.
"We won't be able
to use this planet
if they're here."

"Well, maybe we shouldn't be here,"
I say.
"Maybe the Noburans
have enough planets already."

no WORDS SWAY HIM

Grand Advisor Vorlarus
is unmoved.

"We teach order to chaos,"
he says.
"Because of us,
peace flows from star to star.
You know the code.
You know our way.

Aren't you a Noburan?"

I should be
angry at the question.

But I'm beginning
to wonder if
Noburans might be
as bad as humans.

narvu Doesn't talk

He acts instead.

He grabs the human-child.
The boy, as Vorlarus says.
Shoves him under
his skinny arm.

They speed into
an open tunnel.

Vorlarus raises his band.
Aims his phaser.

Yet chooses
not to fire.

DISBELIEF

Vorlarus let Narvu go.

I'm not sure why.

It's even stranger
to think of my brother
dashing away
with the human-child.

Narvu's never taken
a risk like that
on his own.

I'm kind of proud.

And mostly
terrified
for us all.

BACK ABOVEGROUND IN THE CITY

The humans are
bundled up.
Stacked in piles
by the drones.

There must be
over a hundred.
Squirming in sacks.

The drones keep dipping
into hatches
around the city.
Coming back
with new bodies.

Stacked higher.
And higher.

Pyramids of people.

Pointing toward the smoky sky.

THE SKY IS GROWING DARKER...

"Please!
This isn't right,"
I beg Vorlarus.
"Where are my parents?
Are they even alive?
What are you doing?
What are you going to do?"

Vorlarus doesn't look at me.

He's gazing ahead
at the burning base.

The dome is still untouched.

I can see backup lights
gleaming through the glass.

Night will come soon.

I Can't Stay

When Vorlarus isn't watching,
I bound away.

Past heaps of humans.
Calling out
in their harsh, barky voices.

If the Grand Advisor
sees me sprint,
he doesn't come after me.

He lets me go.
Just like Narvu.

It's almost like
he doesn't care about us.

He wants to get on with
the human hunt.
To prepare the planet
for its new rulers.

AT THE GARDEN DOME

I peer through
a cracked panel of glass.

Inside,
rows of greenery
stand strong.

The Atomic Serpent
hasn't wrecked
the gardens.

The space still holds
the seeds of new life.

I see workers scurry
in the background.
Patching up walls.
Building new barriers.

But there's no sign
of my mother or father.

I ENTER THROUGH A BROKEN PANEL

The workers
are all in gray Gravi-Suits.
The atmosphere
isn't right anywhere.

Figures wiggle
their arms as I pass.
Happy to see I'm alive.

Some point to the med bay.

A place for
the sick and
the dying
and badly hurt.
Tucked in the back
of the dome.

RESTING

My parents are inside
slim silver healing pods.
Plugged into generators.

The Lord and Lady
float in fluid.
Asleep in bright bubbles
and white light.

"What happened?"
I ask a nearby med tech,
pumping chemicals into the pods.

"They were swept into a wall
by some type of explosion,"
the tech says.
"If it even was an explosion.
We don't know what we're dealing with."

"Well, I might,"
I say.

THE RUMBLING RETURNS

The ground quakes again.

Tremors rock
the med bay.

As their healing pods shake,
my parents stay asleep.
So peaceful yet so powerless.

The med tech rushes
to check their vitals.

They're fine.
For now.

The Atomic Serpent
is slithering near us.

And I don't
have a single
glow-spear on me.

THE DOME SHATTERS

Shards from the ceiling
sprinkle over
the ripe rows.

Hanging vines.
Sweet fruits.
Veined petals.
Bright leaves.

Glass falls
like crystal rain
watering the plants.
Twinkling in
the backup lights
against a black sky.

The ground
grumbles
and groans.

The serpent
is here.

A BLINDING BLAZE

It's like a great sun
rising right beside us.

The Atomic Serpent's
diamond tail
flings itself up from
a newly formed crack.

It hurtles toward
the med bay.
Bashing berry bushes
in its way.
Burning through
a line of saplings.

The tip of its tail
tickles the edge
of my mother's pod.
Leaving the red stain
of an afterglow
on the machine.

My parents
might have kept me
out of their projects.

But now I'm involved
in a moment
that their lives depend on.

I can't fail them.

Though I don't know
what to do . . .

OUT OF THE PIT

Up from the chasm
it created
comes the head
of the Atomic Serpent.

It has three eyes
on both sides
of its white-hot face.
Each one is blank and lifeless.
Unaware of the
surrounding chaos.

Fangs of fire flow
from its jagged jaws.

My Gravi-Suit boils.
Melting from
the monster's heat.

The serpent
shimmies toward me.

a BLUR FROM above

The blue of a glow-spear
strikes one
of the serpent's eyes.

The monster lurches back.
Breaking more glass panels
from the dome.

When I look left,
Narvu, the human-child,
and a few other humans
are launching
spear after spear.

They have an entire bundle.
Tied together with fabric
from one of Vorlarus's nets.

My brother tosses
a glow-spear to me.

It's a skilled throw.
Maybe the hologames he plays
are good for his coordination.

Just holding the spear
makes me feel stronger.
Gives me a gush of hope.

The serpent
circles back around.
Teetering as it
winds and weaves.

It's heading
straight toward
the healing pods.

JAB-JAB-JAB

The spear sparks
against the center
of the serpent's head.

Plunging into
the fiery face
that flashes
before me.

Glittering rings
of color
splash across
my visor.

An explosion

    of energy

       knocks me

          on my side.

SPIRALS

Everything
is swirling,
whirling off
into an ocean of white.

I see streaks of blue.

More spears
soar through
my vision.

Then I pass out.

THRUMMING

I wake to
a whir that I recognize.

The buzz of a drone.
Hovering over me.

The Grand Advisor is nearby.

No,
I want to whisper.

I can't speak.

My headset is jammed
in my mouth.

Maybe I'm alive.

But if Vorlarus is here,
then the humans
are done for.

THE DAMAGE

Beyond the fog of my visor,
I see smoke slipping through
what's left of the garden.

Drones bob about
in the misty gray.
Maybe searching
for survivors.
Or more humans
to round up.

The Atomic Serpent
is nowhere in sight.

Tiny fires flicker.
But workers are
putting them out.

The Grand Advisor
is alongside them.
Fighting the last of the flames.

I PUSH MYSELF UP

I brush off my Gravi-Suit.
Adjust the headset.

Limping past injured bodies,
I almost pass out again
before I reach Vorlarus.

"Please . . ."
I mumble.
"The humans saved us.
We'd be dead if it weren't for them . . .
They don't deserve for you to—"

The Grand Advisor
holds up a hand to silence me.

"There's nothing more to say,"
he grins oddly.
"You were right, Nulara.
I understand that now."

THE HUMANS

They're standing
in the smoke
near the med bay.

They're next to Narvu,
who wiggles his arms at me.

His visor is clear.
He's smiling.

The human-leader is there.
No longer strung up in a net.
The creature's crispy cheek-hair
has mostly burned away.

The little boy
is with the group.
Picking at the skin bulge
in the middle of his face.

I'll soon learn to call it a "nose."

TWO
"EARTH MONTHS"
LATER

new uploads

Some humans
once named
this planet "Earth."

My parents let me
access more info
about the human world
through my Illumi-Pillow.

Since then,
I've discovered
Earth's people
had many languages.
Different traditions,
beliefs, and codes.

No wonder they fought so much.

It doesn't take much
for a misunderstanding
to lead to disaster.

I think of the night
we fought the Atomic Serpent.

While hunting for humans,
Vorlarus spied Narvu and the boy
(who has a name now—Jonas).

They were racing alongside others.
Toward the garden dome.
Where the serpent was coiled.

Vorlarus realized their weapons
must ward off the monster.
He journeyed with his drones
to steal the spears.

Then the Atomic Serpent burst beside him.

The humans rescued Vorlarus,
just like they saved
Narvu and me.

Even after everything.

THE FINAL REPORT

In the end,
Vorlarus told my parents
Earth was unsafe for Noburans.

Our royal mission must finish
as soon as possible.

The Lord and Lady were
still healing from their wounds.
They didn't need much convincing.

Vorlarus said the planet
was unsafe for humans, too.

But it was their planet.
They knew it better.
Perhaps they could bring life from death.

They'd shown their potential.

They deserved to stay.

IN THE PAST TWO MONTHS

The workers rebuilt
the garden dome.

We all slept there,
since other parts of the base
weren't worth repairing.

There were no hologames to play.
But I don't think Narvu was bored.

We liked being close to our parents.
Seeing them less as distant royals
and more like family.

We'd proven our worth to them.

So they let us tend to the plants.
To protect what still lived.
To regrow what had been destroyed.

The humans helped us
with repairs.
They lined the dome
with glow-spears.

The Grand Advisor
tried to learn their language.
He wanted to teach them
about the plants.
How to care for them
in the years ahead.

Jonas snuck bites
from the berry bushes.
I don't think he'd ever
tasted anything so sweet.
He got grumpy when
there wasn't extra fruit to take.

He'll need to be
patient with
the plants.
The dome is
for him and
his people.

It's our gift to
the humans.

another chance

We figure if we're leaving,
we can at least
set the humans up
for a better future.

We can't promise
they won't fail.

Their planet is a mega-mess.

Their species might go extinct
no matter what we do.

They'll be replaced
by other lifeforms eventually.
The universe never sits still.

Yet I really hope
the human race
lasts a long time.

ON THE DAY OF OUR TAKEOFF

Jonas gives me
an ashy drawing
he made of us
playing with him.

We're standing
beneath an apple tree
in the garden dome.
Holding hands.

He's made lines
for each of our fingers.

Six-fingered, three-eyed Noburans.
Five-fingered, two-eyed humans.

Hands clasped together.

Friends.

Farewell

We're on our launchpad.
Beside the hulking ship
that brought us to Earth.

A crowd of humans
is there for our final exit.

Parents lift up
their little ones
so they can watch us go.

The human leader
makes a speech
I don't understand.

He's given the Grand Advisor
a glow-spear to study.

Vorlarus still doesn't know
how it works.
But he'll find out someday.

My parents board the ship first.
Many bow to them as they leave.
I guess this is a sign of respect.

Jonas isn't worried about respect.
When I lower my visor,
he tugs on my neck-flaps.
(Which the humans call "ears.")

It still hurts when he does that.

It hurts even more
knowing it's the last time.

The boy wiggles his arms.
He's an expert on the Noburan goodbye.

We wiggle ours back.

As we turn toward the ship,
Jonas hugs our legs.

He doesn't want us to go.

BUT WE DO GO

My family lets me stay awake
for the takeoff.

I can say goodbye to Planet Earth
before settling into
my freezer-bed.

I'm belted beside a window.
Seated with Narvu.
Lost in thought.

I've learned more
from this experience
than from any Illumi-Pillow.

"Hey, meteor-mind,"
my brother nudges me.
"Ready for the next planet?"

We already have
another mission
planned.

LIFTOFF

Before I know it,
we're in the air.
I watch the dome
get smaller and smaller.
Then vanish
in a layer of clouds.

I'm not sure if I'll miss Earth.
But I miss Jonas already.

Space travel is strange.
Especially how it bends time.

Once we reach our next planet,
Jonas will be an old man.

We'll be impossible stories
he tells his grandchildren.

I wonder if his world
will be any better off by then . . .

ON TO OTHER WORLDS

Our ship kicks
into hyperdrive.
Stretching space
so it can rocket
faster than the speed of light.

As the stars swirl around us,
it seems like
we're sailing
on white waves.
Glimmering in
the long dark.

Let peace flow from star to star,
I think to myself.

Maybe some parts
of the old family code
are worth keeping.

Want to Keep Reading?

Turn the page for a sneak peek at another book from West 44 Books:

The Memory Vampires
by Ryan Wolf

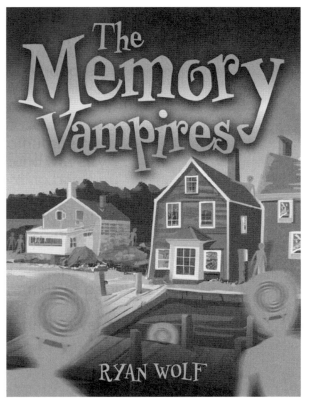

ISBN#: 9781978597211

Part 1
ADAM CARVER

The Other Side of the World

In our backyard
were two rows
of pines.

One row belonged
to our family.
The other belonged
to the people
behind us.

Between the rows
lay darkness
and dirt and
dead pine needles.

My sister and I
used to
play there.

We called it
The Alley.
One summer,
we took shovels
out back.

We wanted to see
how far down
we could
dig a hole.

I hoped we'd find
buried treasure.
A chest left behind
by one of
those colonists
our mom liked
talking about.

Adriana said
she didn't care
about that.

She wanted
to dig deeper.
To get to
the other side
of the world.

"If we dig long enough,
we'll hit
China or Italy
or the ocean,"
she said.

"But isn't the center
of the earth
on fire?"
I asked.

Adriana wasn't
worried.
Explorers must
be brave.
We would put
the fire out
and keep digging.

So we pushed
our spades through
the dead pine needles.
Shoveled until
the ground
got too hard.

Then we went inside
for sandwiches.

When we returned
to The Alley,
the hole
was filled in.

All of our work
was gone.

Our neighbor
probably was
to blame.

But Adriana
claimed
others were
watching us.
People who
knew things.

They filled up
the hole
because they
didn't want us
getting to
the other side
of the world.

I thought about this
as our parents
drove us down
the thruway.

We were heading
to Massachusetts
on a spring break
getaway.

My sister sat
beside me,
earbuds in.
Texting
some boy.

Her golden-brown hair,
the same color
as mine,
caught sunlight
from the window.

She tossed it
aside.

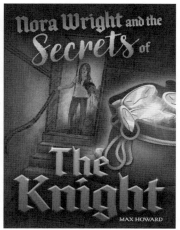

CHECK OUT MORE BOOKS AT:
www.west44books.com

An imprint of Enslow Publishing

WEST **44** BOOKS™

about the author

Ryan Wolf is the author of novels for young adult and middle grade readers, as well as the Creepy Critter Keepers chapter book series for children. He has also published stories, poems, and nonfiction. Wolf holds his B.A. from Canisius College and his M.A. in the humanities from the University of Chicago. His work has been recognized by the Junior Library Guild and nominated for the North Star YA Award. He currently resides in Buffalo, NY, with his wife and two children.